The Big Fire

Rick Sampedro

Illustrated by Giacomo Moresi

Play Station 1

  1 Listen and point.

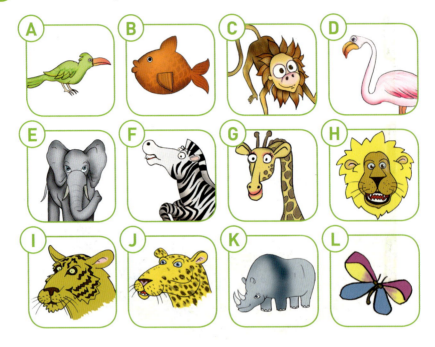

 2 Look at Exercise **1**. Listen and match.

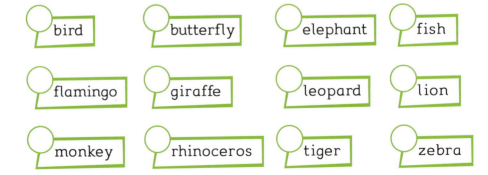

3 Look and circle the correct word.

A There is / are an elephant.
B There is / are three birds.
C There is / are four butterflies.
D There is / are a zebra.
E There is / are a leopard.
F There is / are two monkeys.

4 Listen and check.

Play Station 1

5 Listen and say the chant. Mime the animals.

In the jungle, by the tree, there's a bird.

In the jungle, by the tree, there's a bird and a snake.

In the jungle, by the tree, there's a bird and a snake and a tiger.

In the jungle, by the tree, there's a bird and a snake and a tiger and a giraffe.

In the jungle, by the tree, there's a bird and a snake and a tiger and a giraffe and a monkey.

In the jungle, by the tree, there's a bird and a snake and a tiger and a giraffe and a monkey and ME!

 6 Read and listen to Exercise 5. Draw the jungle picture.

 7 Mime and ask a friend.

 8 Look, listen and tick (✔).

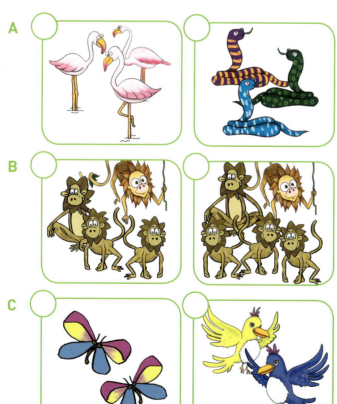

This is the jungle. There are tall trees and cool rivers. The grass is green and the sky is blue. There are lots of animals. They are happy together in the jungle.

Find:
- a leopard;
- a zebra;
- a giraffe.

But the fire is very big and the little blue bird is very small.
There is not enough water in his beak.

Put the sentence in order.
chicks / very / are / scared. / The

But the fire is very big.
And the flamingos are very tired.
They are flying away.
The little birds are alone again.
They are very sad.

What about you?
Tick (✔).

☐ I am happy.
☐ I am sad.

But soon the flamingos are here again.
And there are lots of elephants with them, too.
The little birds are happy again.
They are not alone with the big, big fire.

The fire is big. But there are lots of elephants and flamingos.
They can help the birds. The elephants have water in their trunks and the flamingos and the little birds have water in their beaks. Together they can stop the fire.

This is the jungle.
There are tall trees and cool rivers.
The grass is green and the sky is blue.

Play Station 2

1 Listen and point.

2 Look and match.

The little bird is happy.

The little bird is scared.

3 Look, listen and say.

A 1 B 2 C 3 D 4 E 5
F 6 G 7 H 8 I 9 J 10

4 Look, write and match.

A There are .... flamingos.
B There are .... snakes.
C There are .... monkeys.
D There is .... elephant.

Play Station 2

5 Read and colour.

green
blue
pink
red
orange
yellow
grey
brown   white
black

6 Listen and tick (✔).

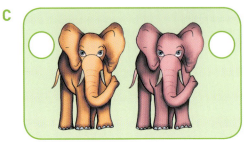

28

 7 Listen and colour.

8 Read and write the numbers.

A How many elephants are there? ....

B How many monkeys are there? ....

C How many snakes are there? ....

D How many flamingos are there? ....

E How many zebras are there? ....

Play Station 2

 9 Look and say.

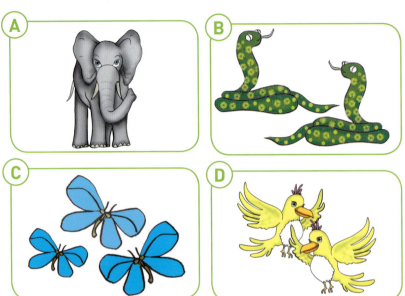

 10 Ask a friend.

11 **Look, write and say.**

A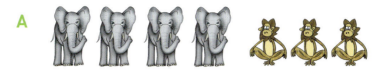

There are four elephants and three monkeys.

B

There are two

C

There

D

E

31

Play Station Project

Jungle dominoes

**Copy the jungle dominoes onto card.
Colour them and play jungle dominoes with your friends.**